Millicent Mary's Surprise

You'll never guess what Millicent Mary found in her garden one winter's day . . . .

Enid Blyton's

Millicent Mary's Surprise

Once there was a little girl called
Millicent Mary. She had a dear little
garden of her own, and in the early
spring the very first things that came up
were the white snowdrops.

Millicent Mary loved them. She loved the straight green stalks that came up, holding the white bud tightly wrapped up at the top. She liked the two green leaves that sprang up on each side. She loved to see the bud slowly unwrap itself, and hang down like a little bell.

But she was always very disappointed because the white bells didn't ring. "They ought to," said Millicent Mary, and she shook each snowdrop to see if she could make it ring. "Bells like this should ring—they really should! Ring, little snowdrop, ring!"

But not one would ring. Still, Millicent Mary wouldn't give up. Every morning when she put on her hat and coat and went into the garden, she bent down and shook the snowdrops to see if perhaps today they would say *ting-a-ling-a-ling*. But they never did.

One day she went to her garden when the snow was on the ground. The snowdrops were buried beneath the snow, and Millicent Mary had to scrape the white snow away very gently to find out where her snowdrops were.

At last all the little white bells were showing. She shook them but no sound came. "Well, you might have rung just a tiny tune to tell me you were grateful to me for scraping the snow away!" said Millicent Mary.

She was just going to stand up and go to the shed to fetch her broom when she saw something rather queer. The snow on the bed nearby seemed to be moving itself—poking itself up as if something was underneath it, wriggling hard.

Millicent Mary was surprised. She was even more surprised when she heard a very tiny voice crying, "Help me! Oh, help me!"

"Goodness gracious!" said the little girl. "There's something buried under the snow just there—and it's got a little tiny voice that speaks!"

She began to scrape away the snow, and her soft, gentle fingers found something small and queer under the white blanket. She pulled out—well, guess what she pulled out!

Yes—you guessed right. It was a tiny pixie, a fairy with frozen silver wings and a little shivering body dressed in a cobweb frock.

"Oh, thank you!" said the pixie in a tiny voice, like a bird cheeping. "I was so tired last night that I crept under a dead leaf and fell asleep. And when I awoke this morning I found a great, thick, cold white blanket all over me—and I couldn't get it off! Just wait till I catch the person who threw this big blanket all over the garden!"

Millicent Mary laughed. "It's snow!" she said. "It isn't a real blanket. You poor little thing, you feel so cold, you are freezing my fingers. I'm going to take you indoors and get you warm."

She tucked the pixie into her pocket and went indoors. She didn't think she would show the fairy to anyone, because she might vanish—and Millicent Mary didn't want her to do that. It was fun having a pixie, not as big as a doll, to warm before the fire!

The pixie sat on the fender and stretched out her frozen toes to the dancing flames. Millicent Mary took a piece of blue silk out of her mother's ragbag and gave it to the pixie. "Wrap this round you for a cloak," she said. "It will keep out the frost when you leave me."

The pixie was delighted. She wrapped the bit of blue silk all round her and pulled it close. "I shall get my needle and thread and make this lovely piece of silk into a proper coat with sleeves and buttons and a collar," she said. "You are a dear little girl! I love you. Yes, really I do. Is there anything you would like me to give *you*?"

Millicent Mary thought hard. Then she shook her head. "No," she said at last. "There isn't anything at all, really. I've got all the toys I want. I did badly want a teddy but I had one for Christmas. I don't want any sweets because I've got a tin of barley sugar. I don't want chocolate biscuits because Mummy bought some yesterday. No—I can't think of anything."

The pixie looked most disappointed. "I do wish you'd try to think of something," she said. "Try hard!"

Millicent Mary thought again. Then she smiled. "Well," she said, "there *is* something I'd simply love—but it needs magic to do it. I'd *love* it if my snowdrops could ring on my birthday, which is on February 13th!"

"Oh, that's easily managed!" said the pixie. "I'll work a spell for it. Let me see—what's your name?"

"Millicent Mary," said the little girl.

"Millicent Mary," said the pixie, writing it down in a tiny notebook. "Birthday, 13th February. Wants snowdrops to ring on that day. All right—I'll see to it! And now goodbye, my dear. I'm deliciously warm with this blue silk. See you again some day. Don't forget to listen to your snowdrops on February 13th!"

She skipped up into the air, spread her silvery wings, and flew straight out of the top of the window. Millicent Mary couldn't help feeling tremendously excited. Her birthday would soon be here—and just imagine the snowdrops ringing!

Won't she love to shake each tiny white bell, and hear it ring *ting-a-ling-a-ling*! Is *your* name Millicent Mary, by any chance, and is *your* birthday on 13th February?

If it is, the snowdrops will ring for you too, without a doubt—so don't forget to shake each little white bell on that day, and hear the tinkling sound they make. What a lovely surprise for all the Millicent Marys!